The First Adventures Of
Roger And
The Rottentrolls

written by Tim Firth
illustrated by Gordon Firth
edited by Robert Howes DISCARD

CHiLDRENS **The** COMPANY Ltd ••• is exactly that

a company formed by friends exclusively for children,

dedicated to providing stimulating material that

both challenges and excites a child's mind

British Library Cataloguing-in-Publication Data. A catalogue record for this
book is available from the British Library.

©1994 International Music Publications Limited
Southend Road, Woodford Green, Essex IG8 8HN, England.

Published by Stave House Publications

STAVE
HOUSE
PUBLICATIONS

THE VALLEY OF THE TROLLS

Exactly why a rocky valley in the most remote backwater of Yorkshire is inhabited by a crowd of two foot high Norwegian Trolls is a complicated story. Everybody knows that all trolls live in Norway, and that most people who live in Norway are in fact trolls. Seven hundred years ago, however, King Arthur's magician, Merlin, was experimenting with weather control when a group of trolls were mistakenly picked up in a large snow cloud and dumped in a craggy ravine just outside the village of Appletreewick in North Yorkshire.

When Merlin appeared on the scene to see whether he had in fact created a snow filled valley to use as the Royal skiing resort, he is reported to have stamped his feet on the ground and shouted 'These rotten trolls have messed it all up' or something similar. Ever since, the trolls have been known as Rottentrolls, and ever since the valley has been known as Troller's Ghyll.

Rottentrolls are about two feet high. They eat wild garlic which they bake into pasties and they wear woollen cardigans spun out of the twizzels of wool left when sheep rub against fences. Apart from this, very little is known about them. I only know so much because I've read this book before. The truth is, no human being has set foot up the Ghyll in all the seven hundred years that the Trolls have been living there, because these cunning little creatures have invented hundreds of ways of keeping people out of their valley. In the early days they just used to throw pebbles at intruders, but after seven hundred years they have come a long way. If

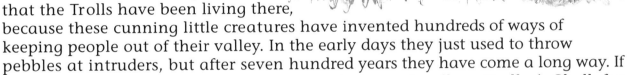

you were to try and walk up Troller's Ghyll, for example, you would firstly find your shoelaces mysteriously tied together. If this did not put you off, and you ventured nearer the opening of the ravine, then you would suddenly be confronted by a sheep with a sign next to it reading *MAN EATING SHEEP*. And if this failed to scare you off (and believe me, few have even made it this far) then a Troll would sprint out from behind a rock, pull a nasty face, and shout, 'There are no toilets for three miles' whereupon you would immediately remember that you desperately wanted to go to the toilet, and rush home.

Now all these nasty tricks are used for one very good reason. Odd as it may appear, the Rottentrolls are not unfriendly, and they are certainly not shy creatures. (In fact a team of trolls recently got through to the semi-finals of a television quiz show in Norway.) The real reason why they won't let anyone in their valley is because they are guarding it.

When the Rottentrolls were first dumped in the Ghyll from Merlin's snow cloud, they looked around to see whose valley it was. Carved into a large rock at the head of the valley were the strange words *Roger was ere*. This, they decided, must be the ruler of their valley, and so for seven hundred years, the Rottentrolls have been guarding the valley until Roger Wasere, whatever he or it might be, returns to take them all back to Norway.

Now Troller's Ghyll is very beautiful. It starts in the Storiths wood at one end, and carves its rocky way up the side of a hill until it peters out a mile further on at the site of a dangerous, derelict, old mine shaft.

The only problem with this beautiful valley, however, is that down that mine shaft lives one of the most terrifying creatures known to mankind. Way down the murky underground caverns of the abandoned coal mine is the lair of the Barguest, a vicious dog the size of a horse with teeth as big as your hand, and eyes the size of dinner plates. Every full moon, the Barguest emerges from its tunnel and stalks down the valley, looking for food. It eats anything, and many trolls have been dragged screaming and kicking off down into the tunnels never to emerge again. Nowadays, no Rottentroll who values his life sets foot outside the cave on a full moon. They all sit, shaking with fear, as the strange screeching howls of the Barguest echo around the desolate valley.

Roger Becket knew nothing of the mysterious, grisly secrets of Troller's Ghyll. He was just eight years old, and for his last birthday he had been given a five-speed racer with special curved handlebars and a strange plastic thing attached to the back wheel. Where Roger lived there was no room to do any cycling, so he had come up to spend the summer holidays at his Grandma's house in Appletreewick. One sunny afternoon, he set off on a long bike ride around the dales. He only got as far as the other side of Appletreewick, however, when the road forked off in two different directions. The signpost pointing to the right read *Skyreholme 1 mile* and pointing to the left it read *Don't go this way.* That road meandered off out of sight between the hills, and looked by far the most interesting of the two to Roger. He got back on his bicycle and rode off down the dusty track.

At the end of the road, Roger got off his bike, opened the gate with *Troller's Ghyll — No entry at all* carved into it, and walked nervously towards the valley. The warm wind rustled the oak trees behind him, but otherwise there was not a sound. The valley looked dark and lifeless to Roger, but of course, he could not see the pair of tiny eyes watching from behind a rock.

As usual, Yockenthwaite was the Rottentroll on guard this afternoon. He was always very eager to help, and so the other Rottentrolls were happy to let him stand guard all the time. He was just about to nip out and tie Roger's shoelaces together, when he stopped dead. Roger, standing at the very entrance to the Ghyll, had decided to shout his name up the valley to see what the echo was like.

'**ROGER** . . . ROGER . . . Roger . . .' His name bounced off every single rock and scuttled off up the Ghyll. Yockenthwaite just stared at the stranger.

'It can't be!' he breathed, swallowing in a big gulp.

'**ROGER** . . . ROGER . . . Roger . . .' shouted Roger again. The echo was so long that Roger decided it was a little too frightening to venture up alone, and turned to leave. Then suddenly he turned back and shouted;

'**Roger was here!**' Then more quietly, 'So there.'

Why he said that we will never know. He was probably just showing off. But whatever the reason, the fact was that he shouted up the valley the very name which the Rottentrolls had been waiting seven hundred years to hear. 'And it's me who found him! Me! Me!' shouted Yockenthwaite. 'I've done something right at last!' With a tremendous spring, he jumped over the rock and landed with a thump on the ground in front of Roger. 'Hello' said Yockenthwaite, not sure quite how he should address the new King of the Rottentrolls.

'Hello' said Roger, not sure quite how he should address a strange two-foot high thing with a woollen cardigan on.

'Is that your bike?' asked Yockenthwaite, staring past Roger down the valley.

'Yes' replied Roger.

'What's that plastic thing on the back wheel for?'

'I'm not sure yet' said Roger. 'I'm Roger by the way.'

'Oh yes I know, I know' said Yockenthwaite, suddenly remembering what he was doing. 'Quick, quick come on.'

Frantic with excitement, he grabbed Roger's hand in his tiny palm, and skipped off up the valley, jumping nimbly from rock to rock, with Roger jumping and stumbling along behind him.

When they finally came to a halt Roger was exhausted, and his shins were covered in bruises.

'That really hurt' he moaned, but Yockenthwaite took no notice whatsoever.

'Aysgarth!' he squeaked. 'Roger Wasere is here! He's come! We're going back to Norway, we're going back to Norway . . .' He started to hop about again, clapping his hands together, when suddenly he was knocked sideways by a large knitted pillow which came hurtling out of the darkness.

'If you don't shut up, now, this minute' said a croaky voice, 'Then I will personally drop you off the top of the Ghyll.'

'But Aysgarth it is, it's him, and I found him, me!' There was a pause, then a sigh, and then the figure of a very wise-looking old Rottentroll emerged out of the darkness. In addition to his knitted cardigan, he had a long, white beard and slippers. He shuffled over to Roger, looked him up and down, and said:

'What is your name?'

'Roger' said Roger.

'And is this your valley?'

'Well, no' answered Roger. Then thinking again, he added, 'Well not really, I suppose it's as much mine as it is anyone else's.'

The old Rottentroll smiled.

'We knew you would come eventually. Oh happy, happy day.' Tears welled up in his eyes. 'Yockenthwaite,' he whispered. 'Go and tell the valley that . . . Roger Wasere is here at last.'

'Roger who?' said Roger.

'I am Aysgarth' said the old troll, bowing his head gently. 'I am ruler of the valley, in your absence. We have waited seven hundred years for you to come from the mists of time.'

'I've come from Carnforth' said Roger, but Aysgarth just clicked his fingers.

'Quick, you must be sworn in as King at once, follow me, follow me up to Trucklecrag's cave.' Roger had given up asking questions. He sighed, and shuffled off after Aysgarth.

The sun was burning down on the rocks as they stepped outside.

'Morning' said a passing sheep. 'Nice weather. Started off a bit chilly. I think I'll have a dip.'

'Good idea' said Roger, who wasn't surprised by anything anymore.

'We taught the sheep to speak many years ago' whispered Aysgarth. 'We needed their help against the Barguest, you see. They're our early warning system.'

'The Bar what?' asked Roger.

'You'll want to know the names of all the Rottentrolls straight away, I presume' mused Aysgarth, ignoring Roger completely. 'Well let's see . . . over there is Kettlewell's cave.' He waved his stick over to the right just as a plumpish troll with a gentle smile appeared.

'How d' you like your garlic pasties, Mr Roger Wasere?' she enquired. The thought of garlic pasties made Roger feel quite sick. 'I don't, really. Sorry.'

'Oh, yes, I suppose you don't really need any magic food to make you live for ever,' she said.

'We eat the wild garlic from Storiths wood' explained Aysgarth. 'My daughter Penyghent picks it, and Kettlewell bakes into pasties.'

'But how do you bake things?' asked Roger.

'In the oven, of course' snapped Aysgarth. 'Garrelgum, our builder, made an oven using heat which comes up from the underground fires'. Garrelgum stepped briskly out into the valley. He was carrying a hammer made out of a rock and a piece of wood. Roger waved nervously at him, and was just about to ask about these underground fires, when a very strange looking troll bounded up. His hair was tousled, and his old cardigan was ripped and ragged.

'It's over there, Norway is, just over the hill!' he squeaked, and then laughed hysterically.

'This is Sigsworthy Crags,' sighed Aysgarth. 'He's completely mad I'm afraid.'

'I'm not mad!' shrieked Sigsworthy Crags indignantly. 'I've built a glider. You can come in my glider and we'll fly away, whee!' Roger stared wide-eyed as he zoomed off up the valley with his arms outstretched, making aeroplane noises.

'It's sad really' mused Aysgarth.

'Yes.' said Roger.

A little further up the valley, Roger noticed a sad-looking, dumpy old troll sitting on a small stone. He seemed to be talking to himself.

'Who's that?' whispered Roger.

'That's Hubberholm' said Aysgarth. 'He once had a daughter called Beckermonds who went missing many years ago now. He went up the Valley of Desolation to find her, and someone or something put a spell on him. He hasn't been able to say a word since. You see that stone he's sitting on?'

'Yes' said Roger. 'He brought that back from his journey. It's called the Noonstone. Every day at Midday he sits on it, and does that . . . it's as if he were talking to someone.'

'What a sad story,' thought Roger, as Aysgarth waved his stick over at the side of the valley.

'That over there is Askrigg's cave. Now Askrigg, he is the strongest and bravest of all the Rottentrolls. You will meet him later, he's taken Strid the Trollslip up the valley for a walk.'

'What's a Trollslip?' asked Roger.

'A baby troll of course, you know that surely' replied Aysgarth.

'Oh yes, of course' said Roger, who didn't.

The pair had only managed another couple of steps when two identical trolls stepped out of nowhere. One was twice the size of the other.

'Oh yes, these are the Nab twins,' said Aysgarth. Great Nab and Small Nab. Great Nab was left out in the rain as a Trollslip and grew to that size.

'He's almost as big as me' whispered Roger.

'Yes, and he's good at knitting too,' added Aysgarth. 'Small Nab collects the wool and Great Nab knits these cardigans for us.' Then Aysgarth dropped his voice and looked around surreptitiously. 'He also made me a knitted cushion on the quiet. It's one of the perks of being ruler. You'll get one too, I suppose.'

'Ah right' nodded Roger, walking off after Aysgarth.

Eventually, Aysgarth stopped, and gestured up to a cave high up in the valley side.

'Up there,' he wheezed, 'Lives Trucklecrag, the magician Rottentroll. He is the one who has to crown you King. He has this thing about talking in riddles too, it's really annoying.'

'Well I don't think he's in anyway,' said Roger, squinting up at the cave.

'No, he's a hermit,' said Aysgarth. 'He just sits in his cave all day. We need the magic password to summon him.' With that, Aysgath gathered all his strength, leaned back, breathed in, and shouted 'Oi!'

'That's not much of a magic password' said Roger.

'It always works,' said Aysgarth, and sure enough, a figure immediately appeared at the mouth of the cave. He looked even older than Aysgarth, and his dark beard was even longer.

'Who has summoned Trucklecrag, magician of the Rottentrolls?' he boomed.

'It's me' said Aysgarth impatiently. 'Roger Wasere has arrived at last from the mists of time. You must crown him King at once!'

'Ah!' said Trucklecrag, lifting up his tiny, wrinkled hands. 'First he must answer the ancient riddle of the Rottentrolls.'

'Oh for crying out loud . . .' whispered Aysgarth, bitterly.

'. . . handed down to me by the Imperial Wizard Merlin seven hundred years ago . . .'

'It wasn't, he's made it up himself' said Aysgarth. 'Get on with it!'

'What,' shouted Trucklecrag in a powerful, serious voice, 'is four feet long, covered in wool, and has four legs!' Roger looked at Aysgarth, who sighed. Then, he looked back up at Trucklecrag.

'A sheep?' he shrugged.

'Correct!' shrieked Trucklecrag, throwing his arms up in the air. 'It is indeed Roger Wasere, come back to us at last! In the name of Merlin and all the Rottentrolls, I crown you Roger, King of the Rottentrolls!'

'No, listen, my name's Roger Becket' said Roger. But nobody was listening.

THE GREAT RESCUE

The sun was gradually slipping out of sight and the stones of the valley were still warm from the heat of the day. A pale crisp full moon slunk out from the clouds and washed Troller's Ghyll in a cool silver light. The new King of the Ghyll was in no mood for enjoying the evening, however. Roger was desperately trying to figure out a way of escaping that night while at the same time listening to Garrelgum, the builder, explain the special throne he had built.

'Y'see' said Garrelgum, broadly. 'You've got this seat bit here, which you sit on, and then attached to that, like, you've got the back bit, which you can lean against. I would have made it more fancy, but you're a bit limited with rocks.'

'It's very nice' said Roger.

'Over there you've got a bed, like, which is a flat rock, and then, being King, you get a desk, which is mostly rock, but it has got wooden legs.'

'Great' said Roger. He was just about to tell Garrelgum to look the other way and make a run for it, when he heard a loud commotion from outside. Aysgarth, his little cheeks bright red with running, scurried in. Yockenthwaite, as ever, was close behind.

'Oh King Roger, King Roger, terrible terrible news! Little Strid got lost when she was out walking with Askrigg, and she went near the mine shaft, and it's a full moon, and the Barguest was out early and he's caught her, he's dragged her off! The Barguest has caught little Strid! Oh terrible, terrible day!'

'Yes' said Yockenthwaite, not very helpfully.

'What is the Barguest?' asked Roger. 'Oh it's terrible, horrible, dreadful' gasped Aysgarth. 'A massive dog with burning red eyes as big as dinner plates. It'll eat the poor little thing up in one bite, we must rescue her.'

'We'll tell Askrigg not to go trying to rescue her alone for a start' said Roger suddenly. 'Bring him here to me.'

'Oh yes, yes, right, right . . .' said Aysgarth, and he scurried off with Yockenthwaite. Roger was quite proud of himself. It was nice to give an order and have somebody do it straight away. For the first time, he actually felt like a King.

Askrigg was pushed into the cave by the Nab twins. He was very good looking (for a troll) and was obviously very strong. He struggled free and bowed briskly to Roger.

'I can't stay King Roger. I have to go and save the Trollslip, it's my duty as the strongest Rottentroll.'

'But the Barguest will eat you up, won't it?' asked Roger.

'Probably' grunted Askrigg.

'Well pardon me for saying' replied Roger, 'but isn't that a bit pointless?' There was a pause. The other assembled Rottentrolls looked serious and nodded their heads.

'There must be a way of getting her back without fighting' mused Roger, scratching his head. 'What is this Barguest again?'

'Oh terrible, awful, horrible . . .' began the Rottentrolls.
'Yes, but what kind of animal is it?' said Roger impatiently.
'A dog,' said Great Nab.
'A horse,' said Small Nab.
'A kind of horsey dog,' said Askrigg. 'With eyes as big as . . .'
'Dinner plates, yes I know' said Roger. 'Look, I think
I've got an idea. I'll go out of the valley . . .'

'Oh no no no!' butted in Aysgarth. 'Oh good heavens, the King can't go out of the valley.'

'One of us must go,' said Askrigg, stepping forward.

'But I need to go to the shop in Appletreewick!' protested Roger.

'You Trolls can't go, Mrs Harris would have a fit! I'll have to go.' A puzzled silence fell over the cave. Everyone thought furiously and hummed and haa-ed. Suddenly, Roger clicked his fingers.

'Got it!' he shouted, taking off his jacket. 'Let's see what it looks like if Great Nab stands on Small Nab's shoulders and they wear my jacket and cycling cap.'

The twins did as he said, and to be honest they looked a little strange, but at a distance, they could possibly pass for a small boy.

'Right, now listen carefully,' said Roger. 'Go down and buy the large-size can of new supervalue Wuffchunks dog food. Don't let Mrs Harris see your faces, and don't whatever you do say anything else. Just say thank you, and leave, alright?' They nodded.

'Now I'm also going to need a piece of string and something to see with down there.'

'I'll get those' blurted Yockenthwaite.

'Oh no you won't' said Aysgarth. 'We can't afford to take any chances. Call Penyghent, tell her.'

'Okay' said Roger. 'Synchronise watches . . .' (he didn't know what this meant, but it sounded good in the films)' . . . and go!'

'Good evening' said Mrs Harris in the village shop.

'A large can of supervalue Woffchunks please,' said the thing with brown feet, a blue jacket and cycling cap over the other side of the counter.

'Certainly,' said Mrs Harris, going to get one off the shelf. 'You're up late, my lad, we were just closing' she added, making idle conversation. The thing in the blue jacket and cycling cap had been told not to make idle conversation, however. It had been told to say one sentence only. So it said it again.

'Ah, a large can of supervalue Woofchunks, please.' Mrs Harris looked puzzled.

'Yes, I've got one for you. Are you alright?' The thing nodded and began to back out of the door.

'Well goodbye then,' said Mrs Harris. 'Thank you for calling.' She saw one little arm stretch out to open the door, and then, to her absolute amazement, she noticed another little brown arm reach out from lower down, about where the young lad's knee should be, and wave at her as the thing disappeared from sight round the corner. Her mouth fell open in amazement as she limply lifted her arm to wave back.

'What do you mean, you waved?' Said Roger angrily when the twins arrived back. 'If you'd been caught, we would never have got the dog food.'

'But she was being so friendly,' said Small Nab, 'It seemed rude not even to say goodbye.'

'Well we got the bait anyway, so that's good,' said Roger.

'Now listen. I'm going to go down the mine to rescue Strid. I'm going to tie this piece of string to my waist, and I want someone to hold on to the other end, so that when I go in, I can find my way out again.' This was Roger's second good idea of the day, and he felt quite proud of it. His voice had grown official and King-like.

'Right, synchronise watches,' he said again, and with a brisk movement, he swept out of the cave.

The night outside was warm. On both sides the rocky valley rose up into the pitch darkness.

'I'll come and hold the string' whispered a voice next to Roger.

'Who is it?' he whispered back.

'Penyghent, daughter of Aysgarth. I've been up to that mine before. Follow me.' Without another word, Penyghent took the torch from Roger and set off up the valley.

'Come on' she beckoned, and Roger followed. Their two shadows flickered across the valley wall towards the far end, where Roger could just about make out the shape of a ramshackle old mine building.

'It lives down there' said Penyghent when they reached the eerie opening.

'Now don't make a sound, and don't let the string come undone.'

'Right' said Roger, who was starting to regret being such a fearless King. 'I'll go down then.'

Penyghent looked up and squeezed his hand. 'Good luck King Roger' she whispered.

The stones down below ground were slippery and cold, and somewhere far off down the tunnel, Roger could hear the crackling of a fire. He climbed down the side of the shaft and had only taken a few steps when the terrible screeching roar of the Barguest hurtled down the tunnel, echoing round and round. Roger threw himself against the wall and froze in fear. He was quite ready to turn back, when he heard a tiny voice mixed in with the roaring echoes of the monster. This must be Strid's voice, he thought.

Gritting his teeth and clenching his fist more tightly round the piece of string, Roger carried on down the tunnel.

The crackling of the strange fire grew louder all the time, and soon Roger began to feel the heat from it. He stopped at a point where the passageway bent sharply round to the right. The heat was now almost overpowering, and a scorching yellow light was leaping and licking in the darkness. Worst of all was the sound of a heavy, rasping growl. This, he decided, must be the lair of the Barguest. Quickly, he checked the string, the torch and the can of dog food in his pocket. Everything was there. Then, with a great intake of breath, Roger turned the corner.

The lair was a massive underground chamber, with bare stone walls, and the most ferocious fire roaring in the middle. The light was blinding, but Roger could just about make out the shape of a little Trollslip perched high on a ledge. For a moment, he thought he saw the shape of another troll dart behind the fire, but he decided he must have been mistaken. The Barguest itself was nowhere to be seen, so without wasting any time Roger raced over to the ledge and seized Strid in both hands. Strid, of course, had no idea that Roger was King of the Rottentrolls. She had never seen a human so close before, and her terrified eyes widened even further with fear.

'It's alright,' said Roger, 'I've come to . . .' Roger stopped dead at the sound of a terrible screeching roar behind him. He turned round.

Out of the very middle of the fire rose the most terrifying creature Roger had ever seen or imagined. It was as big as a horse with large sharp teeth and burning red eyes as large as dinner plates. It opened its jaws, smashed them together again, threw its head back and let out another terrible screeching howl. Roger quickly slipped Strid into his pocket, so that only her eyes were peeping over the edge. Then he brought out the can of dog food.

'Who has dared come to the fire nest of the Barguest?' growled the Barguest, its red eyes flashing round the chamber like red searchlights.

'Roger Becket. From Carnforth,' stuttered Roger.

'You will be devoured with the other one!' bellowed the creature.

'What does devoured mean?' asked Roger, playing for time, but the creature had moved one long clawed foot out of the fire towards him.

'**Devoured**' repeated the Barguest.

'Look, I taste horrible' blurted Roger suddenly. 'Have you ever tried new supervalue Wuffchunks?' He held the can out, his arm shaking.

The Barguest stopped, its fangs dripping. There was a pause. The can had on it a picture of a dog who was clearly enjoying his can of Wuffchunks. The Barguest stared at it. Roger's heart was beating so loudly he could hear it above the noise of the fire. Finally, with a slow, bitter snarl, the Barguest growled.

'**I haven't got a can opener.**'

'Use your teeth' said Roger quickly, rolling the can across towards the Barguest.

'It's delicious, it really is.'

The Barguest paused for a moment. Roger held his breath. Then with a swoop of its mighty head, the beast bent down and seized the can between its four front fangs. Of course, the can punctured immediately, and for a moment the frightening jaws were useless, stuck in a can of supervalue Wuffchunks.

That moment was all that Roger needed. He darted out of the chamber, and along the tunnel, fumbling from wall to wall in the darkness looking for the trail of string. Little Strid clung on for dear life in Roger's pocket. She didn't know who he was, but whoever he was, he was nicer than the Barguest. With the awful screeching roars ringing down the tunnel behind them, Roger pelted towards the mine shaft, and climbed up and out of the dreadful tunnel into the safety of the Ghyll.

He was met not only by Penyghent, still clutching her end of the string with crossed fingers, but by all the Rottentrolls, standing in a ring around the mine shaft with their tiny torches. When they saw Roger's grimy face emerge, they all cheered, but when they saw Strid pull down the edge of Roger's pocket and stare out, they cheered even more. Aysgarth, with a strangely knowing smile, shuffled forwards, lifted Strid out of the pocket and handed her to Kettlewell. Then he turned and looked up at Roger. The little ring of torch fires danced in the warm wind of the Troller's Ghyll night.

'Roger Wasere,' he said quietly, 'You will make a very good King of the Rottentrolls.'

'My name's Roger Becket!' he said, but I don't think anybody heard him.

THE END